SO-AZA-888

For Kayleigh

SIMON & SCHUSTER BOOKS FOR YOUNG READERS

1230 Avenue of the Americas

New York, New York 10020

Copyright © 1994 by Carol Morley.

Originally published in Great Britain by ABC, All Books for Children,

a division of The All Children's Company Ltd.

All rights reserved including the right of

reproduction in whole or in part in any form.

First American Edition, 1995.

SIMON & SCHUSTER BOOKS FOR YOUNG READERS

is a trademark of Simon & Schuster.

Designed by Anahid Hamparian

The text for this book is set in Bernhard Modern Bold.

Manufactured in Singapore

10 9 8 7 6 5 4 3 2 1

Library of Congress Catalog Card Number: 93-87672

ISBN: 0-671-89551-6

CAROL MORLEY

FARMYARD SONG

SIMON & SCHUSTER BOOKS FOR YOUNG READERS

PUBLISHED BY SIMON & SCHUSTER

NEW YORK   LONDON   TORONTO   SYDNEY   TOKYO   SINGAPORE

I had a cat and the cat pleased me,
I fed my cat by yonder tree;
Cat goes fiddle-i-fee.

I had a hen and
the hen pleased me,
I fed my hen by yonder tree;

Hen goes chimmy-chuck,
chimmy-chuck,
Cat goes fiddle-i-fee.

I had a duck and the duck pleased me,
I fed my duck by yonder tree;
Duck goes quack, quack,

Hen goes chimmy-chuck,
chimmy-chuck,
Cat goes fiddle-i-fee.

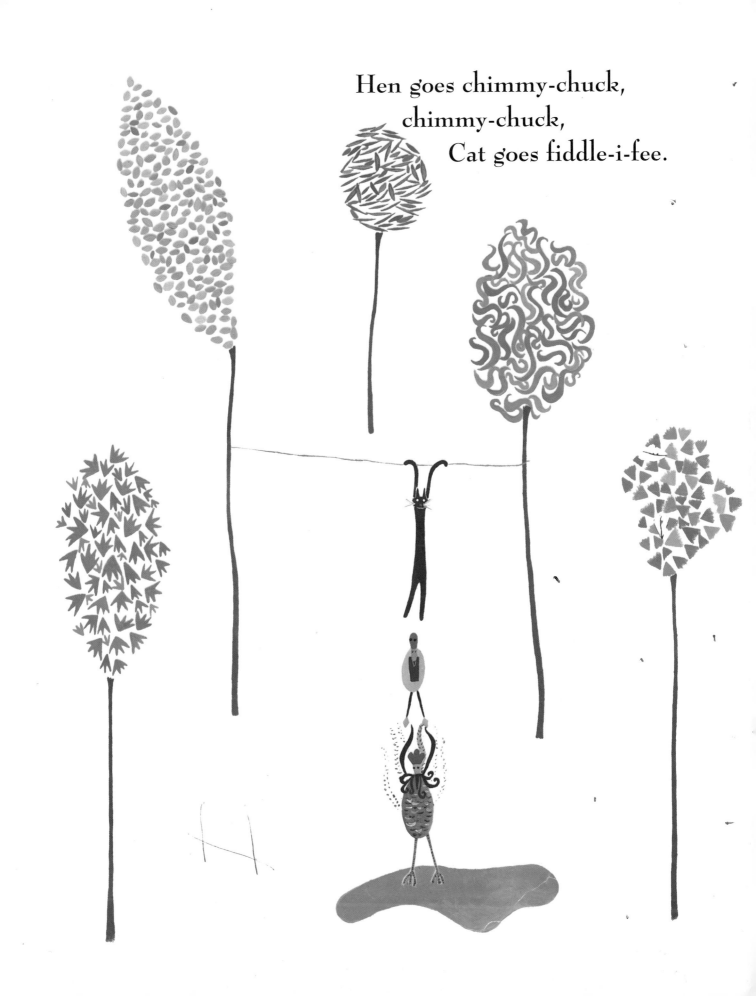

I had a goose and the goose pleased me,
I fed my goose by yonder tree;

Goose goes swishy, swashy,
Duck goes quack, quack,

Hen goes chimmy-chuck,
chimmy-chuck,
Cat goes fiddle-i-fee.

I had a sheep and
the sheep pleased me,
I fed my sheep by yonder tree;
Sheep goes baa, baa,

Goose goes swishy, swashy,
Duck goes quack, quack,
Hen goes chimmy-chuck,
chimmy-chuck,
Cat goes fiddle-i-fee.

I had a pig and the pig pleased me,
I fed my pig by yonder tree;
Pig goes griffy, gruffy,

Sheep goes baa, baa,

Goose goes swishy, swashy,

Duck goes quack, quack,

Hen goes chimmy-chuck, chimmy-chuck,

Cat goes fiddle-i-fee.

I had a cow and
the cow pleased me,
I fed my cow by
yonder tree;

Cow goes moo, moo,
Pig goes griffy, gruffy,
Sheep goes baa, baa,
Goose goes swishy, swashy,

Duck goes quack, quack,
Hen goes chimmy-chuck, chimmy-chuck,
Cat goes fiddle-i-fee.

I had a horse and
the horse pleased me,

I fed my horse
by yonder tree;

Horse goes neigh, neigh,
Cow goes moo, moo,

Pig goes griffy, gruffy,

Sheep goes baa, baa,

Goose goes swishy, swashy,
Duck goes quack, quack,

Hen goes chimmy-chuck,
chimmy-chuck,
Cat goes fiddle-i-fee.

I had a dog and the dog pleased me,
I fed my dog by yonder tree;
Dog goes bow-wow, bow-wow,

Horse goes neigh, neigh,
Cow goes moo, moo,
Pig goes griffy, gruffy,

Sheep goes baa, baa,
Goose goes swishy, swashy,

Duck goes quack, quack,
Hen goes chimmy-chuck, chimmy-chuck,

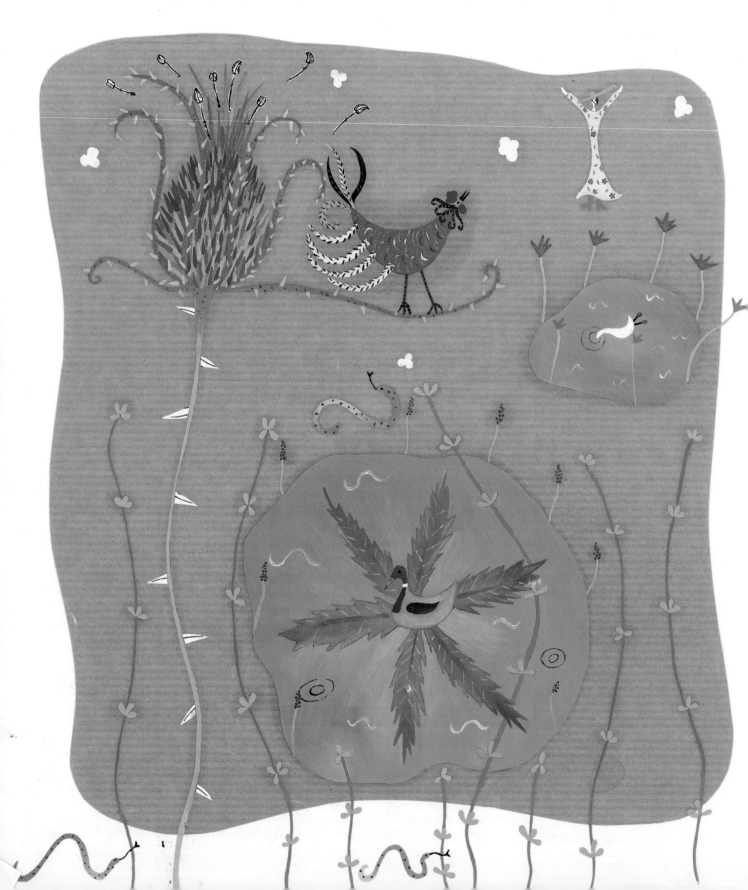

Cat goes fiddle-i-fee.